Editor: Jennifer Schnoes
Cover Design: Studio 52
Author Photo: Adrienne Hatton Mack
Illustrations: Property of Microsoft Corp.

Book Design and Typography
by Adrienne Hatton Mack

FDS Chicago
566 West Adams Street
Chicago, IL 60661
www.fdschicago.com

ed. of 1000 copies

This book was typset in
Times New Roman 12/22
Times New Roman Italics 12/22

Printed in the U.S.A.

Romance Around Chicagoland.
Author: Adrienne Hatton Mack
ISBN. 978-0-615-36543-5

1

Romance Around Chicagoland

To love oneself is the beginning of a lifelong romance.

-Oscar Wilde-

"The first stop on the road to romance is you. Honoring and loving yourself opens the door for another to truly do the same."

Rev. Laurie Sue Brockway

ROMANCE AROUND CHICAGOLAND

BY

ADRIENNE HATTON-MACK

Dedication

To Geraldine Moody for being so positive
and always there…losing you grandma just
didn't seem fair. You left me behind but I'll
be fine….I'll see you again at the end of
time.

Love Always Trece

P.S. Thank you for being so wonderful

Acknowledgments

I would like to thank…

My husband, Derrick, for being a supportive romantic with the willingness to explore all of my endeavors.

My parents, Carolyn and Maurice Jackson for all their support and generosity

And host of friends for their encouraging words and enthusiasm.

A special love goes out to my brothers and sisters for being my motivation and inspiration despite all obstacles.

Contents

Why Romance is Necessary

Romance is a necessary essential to all relationships. Romance is the key component to keep the fire from extinguishing from any loving, healthy relationship. Romance can always lift someone's mood or spirits with kind gestures, thoughts and consideration that can enhance your relationship with minimal efforts in most cases. In my opinion, with romance it's generally the thought or action that counts and not so much the material gifts.

The best romantic surprise I have ever received was flowers at work. No matter how good or bad my day was going, flowers were guaranteed to change my mood from sad to happy or from happy to happier.

Romance will give a relationship its core or foundation. Romance will connect you to your partner; it will help you hear words unspoken and to feel passion and care. Romance makes conversations tranquil which makes it easy to share endeavors and struggles.

Romance will help to saturate your relationship with love and understanding. It acts as a portal for you and your partner to communicate and to share your inner most desires. Romance brings about devotion, a selfless affection and a dedication to your special loved ones.

Romance sets the foundation for all relationships; romance is your soul's introduction to passion, devotion and most of all, love.

You don't have to be a hopeless romantic like myself to be a successful romantic. In my book, you will find several different places around the city of Chicago and its neighboring suburbs all mapped out for you. With my guide to different restaurants, Bed & Breakfasts, spas, theatres and more, being a romantic will be a breeze. All you need is right at your fingertips to get you started on being the best romantic in order to spice up your relationship and to nourish your soul with the essential ingredient for love...Romance.

Restaurants

Remember the old saying "The way to a man's heart is through his stomach."

"There is no love sincerer than the love of food"

[George Bernard Shaw Man and Superman]

Geja's Cafe

340 West Armitage
Chicago, IL 60614
773.281.9101
www.Gejascafe.com

Geja's is one Chicago's most romantic dining experiences, offering fondue dining, fine wines and live classical guitar. Fondue dining features Flaming Chocolate Fondue flamed with orange liqueur and paired with delectable fruit. Also to be reckoned with is Geja's pleasurable Cheese Fondue blended with delicate cheeses, wine, brandy and savory spices paired with lush fruit and other pleasing choices. Moreover, if accompanying you is a large appetite, try out one of the Premier fondue dinners which include the chocolate and cheese fondue appetizer. Wallow in the intimacy of the atmosphere and spoil your date with the sounds of a live guitarist.

Reservations are highly recommended.

SEE COUPON SECTION FOR DISCOUNT

Coopers Hawk Winery & Restaurant

15690 S. Harlem Avenue
Orland Park, IL
708-633-0200
www.chwinery.com
There are several locations throughout the Chicagoland area. Please visit the website for hours, locations and contact information nearest you.

Coopers Hawk has a contemporary atmosphere designed for a sensual and casual romantic experience. While enjoying a modernistic ambience with up-to-date streaming music, you may tour their tasting rooms and sample some champion wines. Conclude your experience with several food and wine combinations on the menu which are sure to satisfy your palate and arouse your senses.

SEE COUPON SECTION FOR DISCOUNT

Signature Room at the 95th

875 N. Michigan Avenue
Chicago, IL
(312) 787-9596
www.signatureroom.com

Located at the top of the John Hancock
Center, The Signature Room's romantic
attributes includes its scenic views of the
cities glistening, twinkling lights. Couples
can enjoy a fine contemporary cuisine from
steak and potato cake to a roasted rack of
lamb illuminated by a candle lit table all the
while relishing in the sounds of live piano
and music.

Chicago Elegant Dinner Cruise

Chicago, IL
888-881-3284
www.chicagotours.us

Get all dress up and take a three hour tour of Chicago's dazzling skyline while enjoying dancing, live music, and delectable menu items. There are three dining rooms all attractive and pleasing to sight, charmingly decorated with linen table clothes, alluring dance floors, a live band and piano. Be sure to go onto the deck to view the sky above blanketed with stars.

Cite'
Lake Point Tower
505 North lake Shore Drive
Chicago, IL 60611
312-644-4050
www.Citechicago.com

Cite' is an elegant restaurant with romantic surroundings of downtown Chicago. It canvases 360- Degree scenic wide ranging views of Chicago's lakeshore and Chicago's skyline from the top of Lake Point Tower. Aside Cites' all-encompassing views and romantic atmosphere, the menu is a succulent delight.

Less Expensive Alternative....

Instead of going out to dinner make dinner at your home, by creating a different atmosphere and preparing the food yourself, your creativity and your efforts are sure to win you major brownie points!!!
First start by sending your partner a letter or email letting them know that you are taking them to dinner indicate time and location (your living room, kitchen etc) and tell them to dress casual but not too relaxed. Then go on to choosing their favorite foods and then making a menu (get the menu laminated to look more professional).Also include a small picture of yourself on the menu next to the name of the restaurant (that way your partner can take the menu as a keepsake).Make sure your menu includes a house salad and bread of some sort. Put a choice of two appetizers, two side dishes with two main course entrée's.

Include three choices of cocktails (each named after your partner or something special about the relationship and change the labeling on the bottle). Include a choice of two desserts, one you made and ice cream of choice. Make sure your table is covered with a nice fabric table cloth and napkins and use nice candles as your centerpiece, along with nice ground salt and pepper shakers. Make sure there is soft smooth music playing in the background. Have a friend or family member serve you dinner in your home.

Bed & Breakfasts

Whether it's the birth of a new relationship or to revitalize a current one, a Bed & Breakfast getaway is a great way to escape the fast paced and busy activities of your everyday lives to rejuvenate or connect with your special someone.

The greatest thing you'll ever learn is to love and be loved in return.
~ From "Unforgettable with Love" by Natalie Cole

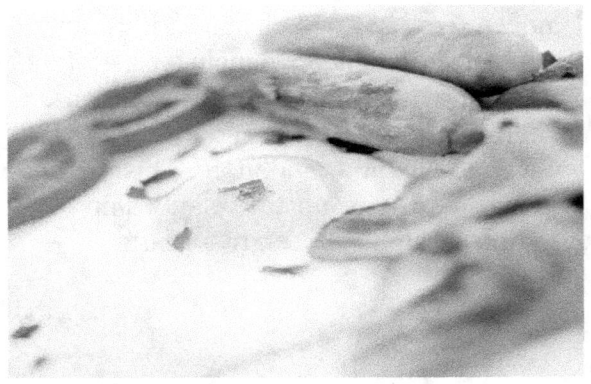

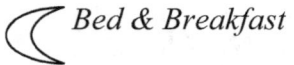

Old Town Chicago Bed & Breakfast inn
1442 N. North Park Avenue
Chicago, IL, 60610
Phone: 312-440-9268 Fax: 312-440-2378
www.oldtownchicago.com

Old Town Chicago B&B is an extravagant, accommodating Bed & Breakfast, equipped with a contemporary charm in a community surrounding. Each of the suites comes with a queen sized bed and en suite bathroom. Shared accommodations includes a 45 foot long living/dining room, rooftop gardens, a penthouse sitting area, workout rooms, convention exhibits and more. This romantic inn is sure to spice up any relationship igniting passion between two hearts.

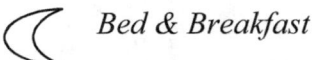

Windy City Sailing/Bed & Breakfast
3400 Recreation Drive
Chicago, IL. 60613
773-868-0096
312-242-1745 cell
www.windycitysailing.com

Enjoy an invigorating, memorable experience of a bed and breakfast on a secluded yacht. Take pleasure in a sail around Chicago's lakefront while enjoying a delightful breakfast for two. After a night's view of glistening waters, glowing lights nestled under a star filled sky in quarters constructed for pleasure.

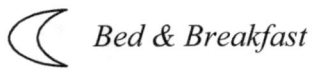

Harvey House Bed & Breakfast
107 South Scoville Avenue
Oak Park, IL 60302
708-848-6810
708-955-7254 Cell
www.harveyhousebb.com

Filled with serenity and tranquility, the
Harvey House Bed & Breakfast offers a
peaceful mood and soothing atmosphere
with first class offerings and high end décor.
Be sure to reward yourself with a
therapeutic massage and some savory
chocolates. An elaborate breakfast, made to
order, awaits you at sunrise.

SEE COUPON SECTION FOR DISCOUNT

20

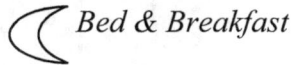

Rays Buck Town Bed & Breakfast
2144 North Leavitt
Chicago, IL 60647
773-384-3245
www.raysbucktownbandb.com

At Rays Buck Town B&B, a couple nights'
stay is sure to keep the doctor away.
Rejuvenate in the steam room or revitalize
in the sauna. Either is sure to exhilarate
your mind and body. Unwind and relax in
the whirlpool tub and step out onto a heat
floor. The Da Vinci room is what I most
adore.

In the morning your breakfast is made to
order.

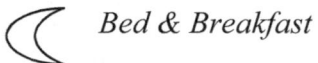

Lynfred Winery

15 South Roselle Rd.
Roselle, Illinois 60172
United States
630-529-9463
http://www.lynfredwinery.com

Lynfred Winery is a charming retreat with subtle elegance and ravishing essence. Offering exquisite wine country themed accommodations complete with whirlpool tubs and burning fireplaces, coupled with accomplished vintages, wine tastings and superior service. Be sure to take advantage of their complimentary weekend wine cellar tours offered January through October.

SEE COUPON SECTION FOR DISCOUNT

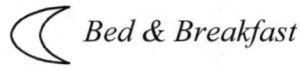

Less Expensive Alternative....

Invite a couple to stay in your guest bedroom. Decorate the bedroom in different themes using removable wall decals, pictures, flowers, a bed canopy, candles, seashells, rose petals and so forth.

Examples: Hawaiian Luau room or seashell beach themes for a staycation getaway—find décor at your local dollar store or party supply store. Be sure to pick up a CD (to match the theme of the room) for your guests' listening pleasure. Make a sign for the door to the guest bedroom naming the suite (ex: Hawaiian retreat or Seashell Shore.)
Include: A fruit basket in the guest room with a thank you for joining us card attached. A small refrigerator (a small cooler filled with ice will do fine) stocked with juice, soda, bottled water and a bottle of wine/champagne is a nice touch. Make sure the room is equipped with an ice bucket,

Glasses, television, CD player, DVD player and three movies and CDs to choose from. Also include towels (in three sizes) soap, toothpaste, toothbrushes, a comb and brush (in trial sizes) neatly arranged in a small basket. If you invite guests often, remember to replace these items with each passing guest.

Enjoy an evening of charades, karaoke, and movie watching with your guest and let them retire to their elaborately decorated retreat providing them with a small gift bag of sex novelties to enjoy the duration of their stay.

Be sure to take their menu request that evening to cap off the morning with a made to order delightful breakfast.

Dinner Theaters

Looking for a movie theatre with a twist?
Chicagoland houses some of the most
exciting, romantic, charming and
entertaining dinner theaters in the Midwest.

*"The most precious possession that ever
comes to a man in this world is a woman's
heart."* ~ by Josiah G. Holland ~

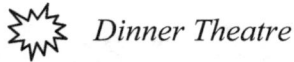 *Dinner Theatre*

AMC Premium Cinema & Restaurant
80 Yorktown Center
Lombard, IL 60148
630-495-0048

An upscale movie going experience satisfying to sight and romantically obliging, this cinema & restaurant has a classy romantic atmosphere. The lobby is an impressive experience all on its own, designed like a cocktail lounge with conversational table seating; an appealing stocked bar, soft lighting and superior wait staff. The theatre rooms are small and intimate with fashionable, comfortable leather seating designed for you to dine and watch the BIG screen. This upscale movie going experience will be pleasingly entertaining for both you and your date.

Showcase Icon Theatre
150 W. Roosevelt Road
Chicago, IL 60605
312-775-3160
www.showplaceicon.com

Enjoy a lobby lounge environment at this cutting-edge theatre, furnished with red leather seating and all digital projection screens. The Showcase Icon Theatre is truly an immeasurable cinema adventure, fully equipped with a bar and upscale appetizers.

 *Dinner Theatre*

Tommy Gun's Garage Theatre
2114 S. Wabash
Chicago, IL 60616
312-225-0273
www.tommygunsgarage.com

Surrounded by 1920s collectibles and the sounds of 1920s music, you are sure to take a nostalgic trip back in time to the roaring twenties with Al Capone and his mafia family at Tommy Gun's Garage Theatre. Join the fun as the staff puts on a phenomenal performance and gives great service as you watch, dine and offer audience participation in this musical comedy.

SEE COUPON SECTION FOR DISCOUNT

Murder Mystery Dinner

773-267-6400
Mysteryltd.com
Call or visit the website for specific details
and locations.

Whether in a mansion or on a train, a murder
mystery dinner will to be an entertaining
delight. Stay engaged as murders will occur
while you dine and move about. See if you
can be the first to figure the murderer out.

 *Dinner Theatre*

Hollywood Palms Cinema & Eatery
352 South Route 59
Naperville, IL 60540
630-428-5800
http://www.hollywoodpalmscinema.com

This cinema has a picturesque essence, exquisite demeanor and a graceful appearance. It encompasses cascading waterfalls, extensive greenery and themed cinema rooms ranging from an 800 gallon saltwater reef aquarium with beautiful fish to be found in the Blue Auditorium as well as an Egyptian Palace featuring the Royalty of the Nile and the Gods in the Gold Auditorium. All the auditoriums are equipped with high back leather chairs and wait staff eager to serve you.

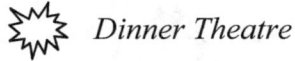 *Dinner Theatre*

Less expensive alternative....

Let's take it back to when going to the movies were all about the Junk Food!!!

First send your loved one a personalized movie theatre invitation by mail or email (example on the next page...feel free to cut out).

Next, go to the store for supplies.

1 Pkg. of Hotdogs
1 Pkg. of Hotdog buns
Hot dog trimmings such as onions, relish, tomatoes, pickles, ketchup & mustard
1 Popcorn container something that reads popcorn (try your local dollar store)
1 Bag of popcorn (microwave is fine)
6 Boxes of assorted theatre candies (buy at local candy store, Walgreens or dollar store)
Soda Pop & 1 Bottle of Wine

☼ *Dinner Theatre*

*Have trimmings for the hotdogs diced &
prepared in separated dishes and set up
buffet style.*

*Surprise him/her with a new DVD that
they wanted to see but never had a
chance to or something they have been
looking for but couldn't find on DVD (do
some investigating to find out what that
might be). Find a poster of the movie
(visit your local music stores, book store
or try ordering it online.) so they
could have it as a keepsake also.*

*Make this experience all about your
date's favorites the movies, candies,
trimmings and so forth. Keep in mind we
are trying to impress. For a fraction of
the cost and tremendous effort this is
sure to be an impressive date.*

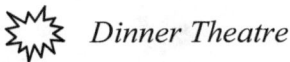 *Dinner Theatre*

Dinner Theatre Coupon

Love & Romance Presents.....
An Evening Together

Featured Movie:

_____

Location:

_____

_____

Date: _____

Time: _____

General Admission: *$ One Kiss $*
All seating is general admission

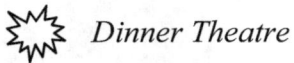 *Dinner Theatre*

Dinner Theatre Coupon

Love & Romance Presents.....
An Evening Together

Featured Movie:

_____

Location:

_____

_____

Date: _____

Time: _____

General Admission: _$ One Kiss $_
All seating is general admission

Chicago Tours

Walk, taste, or ride along for one of
Chicago's most exciting romantic tours
which is sure to excite, entice and delight.

*"One does not fall into love; one grows into
love, and love grows in him/her."*
~ by Dr. Karl Menninger~

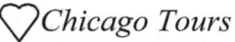

Chicago Chocolate Tours

333 N. Michigan Avenue, Suite 932
Chicago, IL 60601
312-929-2939
info@chicagochocolatetours.com
www.chicagochocolatetours.com

Chocolate is a sweet way to romance any date, so come along for an educated, delectable, aromatic 2 ½ hour walking and tasting tour of Chicago's chocolate shops and bakeries. Smell the aromas and taste the treats as you sweep your date off their feet.

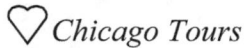

Chicago Horse & Carriage Ltd.

NW corner of Pearson St & Michigan Ave.
Chicago, IL
773.395.3950
info@chicagocarriage.com
www.chicagocarriage.com

Take an evocative Horse & Carriage ride
tour and choose your route from several
Chicago landmarks and neighborhoods. Be
sure to inquire about the additional
supplements to customize your tour to
induce intimacy.

Bike and Roll Chicago
Bike@Nite Tour

There are several starting point locations throughout the downtown Chicago area. Please call or visit the website for hours, locations and reservation information.

773-729-1000 or 888.BIKE.WAY
info@bikechicago.com
www.bikechicago.com

Biking at night is surely a pleasure: this experience is one to be treasured. Chicago's attractions are radiant and brilliant making the evening fun and resilient. After the ride, come along for a boat tour and watch the skyline in its beautiful decor. Cuddle close as fireworks dazzle the sky above; this is a night your date would love.

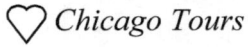

Waterides/Chicago Kayak Tours
950 N. Kingsbury Street
Chicago IL 60610
312-953-9287 wateriders@gmail.com
www.wateriders.com

Relish in scenic views and listen to
historical tales as you "row, row, row your
boat gently down the stream." Glide
through the waters at twilight, for the
fireworks are a sure delight.

This trip is for the audacious and
adventuresome. Be sure to check with your
mate before you book a date.

 *Chicago Tours*

Chicago Food Planet Food Tours

1600 N. Damen Ave.
Chicago, IL 60647
212-209-3370
www.chicagofoodplanet.com

The paths are off route as the stores are obscured. Let Chicago Food Plant help you find the way through a three hour food tasting tour. You'll have the liberty of visiting a variety of six or seven locations - from Pizzerias, gourmet chocolates and cheeses, teas houses, pastry & desserts while gaining the knowledge of some of Chicago's great 'foodie' neighborhoods.

 *Chicago Tours*

Less expensive alternative.....

Take your date on a personalized site seeing tour with you as the guide. Take them anywhere of your preference around Chicagoland (have the day planned), study up on informative facts and history of the places you will be touring (your date will surely be impressed with your knowledge). Make certain to arm yourself with enough knowledge to be able to answer questions should your date ask. Be sure to stop off at a gift shop or outdoor vendor to pick up a memorable token of your day together. At the end of your tour, whisk them away to a private romantic picnic for two, prepared by you. Pack the trunk of your car without them knowing or pack a backpack to carry along with you (include a cooler with some ice to keep food chilled;

if using a backpack include some icepacks that are well secured.) Make sure you have preselected the picnic area in close proximity to your toured location.

Suggested places to research and tour:

Chicago City Landmarks
egov.cityofchicago.org/Landmarks

The Magnificent Mile
(North Michigan Ave)
www.themagnificentmile.com/history

Chicago Beaches
en.wikipedia.org/wiki/Chicago beaches

Chicago Millennium Park
www.millenniumpark.org/parkhistory

 *Chicago Tours*

Items needed for a romantic picnic:

1 blanket
1 bottle of chilled sparkling cider
Note: Chicagoland prohibits the public
consumption of alcohol in its parks.

2 wine glasses
Bottle opener

4 prepared sandwiches
(2 sandwiches will be fine if large
enough or bought from a sub port)

Condiment packages
Napkins

 *Chicago Tours*

Salad for two (any kind will do, including potato salad, pasta salad or a side salad)

Fresh fruit or vegetables of any kind (Mixed fruit or a Veggie platter is ideal)

Paper plates
Plastic eating utensils
Bottled water for two

Jarred candle and rose petals (silk or satin will do) for a center piece.

Spas

Life is about emotions and emotions depict
our mood; spas are calming environments to
help you unwind and sooth. Leave your
bags on the floor and leave life's stresses at
the door as you enter one of Chicago land's
spa sanctuaries that is full of tranquility and
relaxation, you'll get all you need and more.

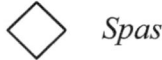 *Spas*

Kohler Water Spa
775 Village Center Dr
Burr Ridge, IL 60527
630-323-7674
www.destinationkohler.com

Hang out all day in your bathing suits as
this water enhanced spa captivates and
rejuvenates you from head to toe. Enjoy a
soft caress from the whirlpool jets.
Adjoining is the waterfalls to knead your
shoulders and neck. Relax in the sauna or
steam room; it will change your mood to
happy from gloom. Retire to a secluded,
private room for calmness and a couple's
massage. Clear your mind of ill thoughts
while thinking only of a happy mirage.

 Spas

Body & Soul Spa
1337 N. Ashland Ave
Chicago, IL 60622
773-276-9722
www.bodyandsoulspas.com

Indulge in a reserved Jacuzzi soak for two.
Talk and unwind while the stress built up
quickly melts away. Get a satiating massage
in separate rooms apart, assured to heal your
soul and feed your heart. Meet again for
more indulgences together, and as you leave
you'll feel light as a feather.

 Spas

Windy City Massage
Chicago, IL
312-946-3000

Will travel to wherever you are to make sure all your needs are met.
Open 7 Days a Week for your convenience
www.windycitymassage.com

Contact them or visit their website for locations and availability

Invite a guest for a couple's massage in your home; be sure to rid of all distractions including the telephone. Complete with all essentials they will arrive within an hour from request; when they leave you will no longer be stressed, you will, however, be very impressed.

SEE COUPON SECTION FOR DISCOUNT

 *Spas*

Lincoln Park Massage Spa

630 W. Webster Ave
Chicago, IL 60614
773-296-6300
www.lincolnparkmassage.com

Escape to paradise while relaxing in a theme filled room for two. Enjoy a couple's massage leaving you feeling rejuvenated and anew. Next is the facial massage to beautify your skin and remove rough patches to show your beauty from within. When you leave you'll feel polished and refined like a new person with all the old left behind.

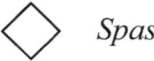

Veola's Day Spa & Wellness Center
2150 West 95th Street
Chicago, IL 60643
(773) 233-1304
www.veolasdayspa.com

Receive pleasure by spending the day together in more ways than one; kick up your heels, lay back, relax and have some fun. Blow her a kiss as you go in a separate direction. It's a symbol of your love and an act of your affection. An exfoliating body scrub awaits her and a jetted tub soak for him; rejoin for a couples massage and end with a nail trim.

SEE COUPON SECTION FOR DISCOUNT

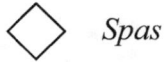 *Spas*

Less Expensive Alternative....

Whether you're the giver or receiver it's a win, win situation when it includes an at home spa!

First: Give your date a spa coupon stating good for one day only. Make sure you indicate the date, time and location. Tell them to come showered and be prepared for a full body satisfaction.

Get Prepared: have a light snack tray of fruits, veggies, chips and small sandwiches (not too heavy a meal, you can eat dinner later)
Beverages: Tea, or wine for calming.

Supplies: Music (soft), red/ pink light bulb, candles, towels (a lot), long sturdy padded table or padded floor for massage and 2 small tables/trays

Have two separate areas prepared for the facial/ manicure and massage.

 *Spas*

Facial station: one chair, 2 small tables or tray filled with supplies & candles for décor, and an additional tray for steam treatment & manicure.

Facial supplies: cleanser, toner, scrub, mask and moisturizer. Also some essential oils: peppermint, lavender, lemon or rosemary oils for problem or oily skin; roses, jasmine, orange or chamomile for dry skin. Always stand behind your subject, towering over when giving a facial.

Facial: Place a warm, damp towel on the face for about 2 minutes.

While you're waiting, put on a pot of boiling water, add a few drops of the essential oils you selected for skin type.

Remove the towel from your love's face and cleanse the skin with the chosen cleanser for skin type.

 *Spas*

*Apply the cleanser gently to the face in a
delicate circular motion; remove cleanser
with a warm towel.*

*Remove the pot from the stove and place it
on a table in front of your subject. Drape a
dry towel over their head and bend their
face over the steam for 5 minutes.*

*Put on the mask: in a gentle, circular motion
apply the mask, add cucumbers over the
eyes. Allow mask to dry. Thoroughly
remove the mask with a hot towel or by
rinsing. End with toner (use a cotton ball to
rub over face) and moisturizer. Keep clear
of your subjects eyes!*

*All supplies can be purchased at your local
drug store for less than $5.00 each.
Essential oils you can purchase at your
local health food store.*

*Manicure Station: same as facial
Supplies: Manicure kit, bowl*

 *Spas*

Manicure: soak their hands in a bowl of warm to hot water for 5-10 minuets

Dry hands and file nails in one direction only.

Trim nails with nail trimmers if desired (cut straight across)

Push back cuticles and clean the nails with a cuticle pusher.

Use a nail buffer to smooth the nails.

Apply the hand scrub, then rinse hands clean.

Massage a drop of essential oil to the base of each cuticle.

Massage the hands with a moisturizing lotion. Wipe the nails clear of lotion and apply polish if desired.

 *Spas*

*Read a book regarding massage techniques
or take a massage class (see page 97)*

*However a gentle or firm back rub with a
massaging oil or lotion is a great
substitution.*

*Massage: On a towel/blanket padded
Sturdy table or floor mat, Have your partner
lie on their belly and stand or kneel beside
them.*

*Start with: right leg and foot, left leg and
foot, back, shoulders and arms. Turn your
partner face up; start with shoulders, chest,
left arm and hand, right arm and hand, and
then end with the left leg and foot and right
leg and foot.*

*Please note: These are suggestions only. Please use
common sense with products meant for skin, and
massage techniques. The author is not responsible
for injury sustained by following these suggestions.*

Air Adventures

Love is in the air….Either planting a seed for a new romance or cultivating the current, going on an enchanting Chicago air adventure surely will arouse emotions promoting intimacy and togetherness.

"We love because it's the only true adventure." --Nikki Giovanni

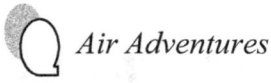 *Air Adventures*

Aviation Vacations/Flightseeing Airplane Dinner Flight

415 North Aberdeen Avenue #200
Chicago, IL 60622
800-757-6603
www.aviationvacations.us

Origination Point:
Midway Airport
5700 S. Cicero Ave.
Chicago, IL 60638

Have yourself a ball viewing Chicago's skyline by dusk or nightfall. See this brilliant, lustrous and romantic city by night and bring a date on an extraordinary, private airplane flight. I hope you have an appetite as later you will retire to Francesca's On Taylor for a multi-course family style dinner for two. This date will serve as a refresher for old love or fertilization for a new.

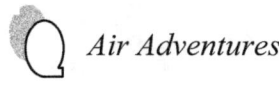

Navy Pier/Ferris Wheel
600 East Grand Ave
Chicago, IL 60611
312-595-7437
www.navypier.com

Nothing says romance like a subtle swing on an old fashion Ferris wheel ride. Catch up and cuddle while swirling around viewing the town. Or say nothing, swinging in silence hand in hand admiring scenery across Chicago land. Either way is a sure treat because this experience is really neat.

 *Air Adventures*

Palwaukee Flyers/Lake Geneva Getaway
1040 S. Milwaukee Ave.
Wheeling, IL 60090
800-901-0730
www.palwaukeeflyers.com

Impress your date by learning to fly and ascend over 2,500 feet off the ground up high. You'll soar over cities and bodies of water in the back watching, she'll be glad you brought her! As you maneuver the aircraft and land on the ground take her to lunch or dinner in a great town.

SEE COUPON SECTION FOR DISCOUNT

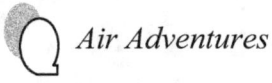

Chicago Helicopter Charter & Tours
Please visit their website or call for additional information
800-615-1655
chicagohelicoptercharters.com

Enjoy a helicopter ride around the city skies and enjoy the views of Chicago's great buildings and high rise. View the lake as your breath it will take, bring a mate and make it a date. Try going late when the cities aglow certain to tickle the fancy of your beau. Steal kisses from your mate; as memories you create this experience is so immeasurable one cannot rate.

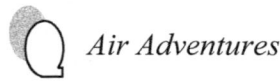 *Air Adventures*

Chicago Hot Air Balloons/Romantic Balloon Flight
Please visit their website or call for
additional information
Chicago, IL
312-854-1879
www.chicagohotairballoons.com

Tour the sky and watch birds fly as the hot
air balloon rises up high. Indulge in a
tranquil environment fully equipped with
serenity and scenery; appreciate the acres of
beautiful land, full of grace and greenery.
Embrace your partner as you sway along
and listen to the melody of the bird's song.

The sky is beautiful and the weather is great;
thank your mate for a wonderful date.

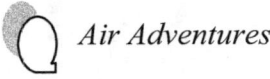 *Air Adventures*

Less Expensive Alternative.....

If you or your date has a fear of heights (or plummeting) and you're not quite the adventuresome type, enjoy a similarly exhilarating experience from earth's surface by visiting Chicago's lakefront for spectacular performances at Chicago's Air and Water show. Two days of fun-filled, adrenaline pumping excitement soars above and sails the sea (lake) while spectators watch in awe. You'll hear roaring sounds of military and civilian jets as they maneuver the skies and dazzle the audience with their action packed performances and fascinating stunts. Lake Michigan is full of boats and water sports, so watch in glee, but also behold the beauty of the lake as far as the eye can see.

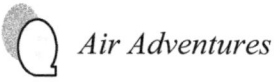 *Air Adventures*

Location:
North Avenue Beach
1600 N. Lake Shore Dr.
Chicago, IL 60610
312-744-3315
www.chicagoairandwatershow.us

Visit their website for additional information for times & dates are subject to change.

Pack a picnic and sun blockers for a joyful day on the beach

Admission: Free
Date: 8/14/2010 – 8/15/2010
Time: 10am-4pm (please arrive before 8am for good seats)

Wine Bars

Swirl, smell, swish and swallow your way
around some of Chicago land's most
romantic wine bars.

*"In water one sees one's own face; But in
wine one beholds the heart of another"
French Proverb Quote*

 *Wine Bars*

The Tasting Room Chicago
Randolph Wine Cellars
1415 W. Randolph St.
Chicago, IL 60607
312-942-1313 or 312-942-1212
www.thetastingroomchicago.com
www.randolphwinecellars.com

Settled in downtown Chicago, The Tasting Room has a warm and intimate interior including candlelit tables, plush seating and a pleasing tone. They offer an extensive collection of wines from several regions , and pair them with small entrees and appetizers. Sip your wine and have conversation on a lush couch or lavish chair. Be engulfed by your surroundings and romance in the air. Go to the second floor and toast with your girl while overlooking a breathtaking view of Chicago's intimate world. Might I suggest you try a wine flight for samples of red and white; step next door to the wine cellar and purchase her favorite of the night.

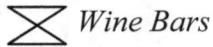

Pops for Champagne
601 North State Street
Chicago, IL
312-266-7677
www.popsforchampagne.com

Like a little effervescence with your grape?
Look no further than Pops for Champagne
with over 100 bottles of champagne and
sparkling wine in this two level house of
bubbly.

Centered in beautiful downtown Chicago
and outfitted in a transparent exterior where
you can admire some of the incandescent
city at night. Accessorized in casts of amber
and gold, while bubbly structures frame the
walls and the upstairs bar made of lucid
natural onyx and amber. The lower level is
a Jazz Club where you can enjoy live jazz
from some of Chicago's first rate musicians
seven nights a week, decked in exposed
stone walls, mellow lighting and lowered
ceilings reminiscent of an underground
Parisian jazz club of the 1920s. Also, try
some of their exquisite champagne food
pairings and desserts.

SEE COUPON SECTION FOR DISCOUNT

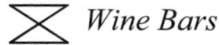

Juicy Wine Company
694 N Milwaukee
Chicago, IL 60622
312-492-6620
www.juicywine.com

Luxuriate in a loft-like lounge environment accented with exposed brick walls, hardwood floors and dashing wall art. This place oozes wine, cheese and intimacy all housed in a dimly lit, chic domain with cheese plates and a variety of wines to choose from. Nestle in a plush, round booth together watching old movies on the flat screen televisions or talk amongst each other singing along or listening to the sounds of a live DJ.

Visit the patio when the weather is warmer, where the scenery is full of vegetable growing planters.

D.O.C Wine Bar (Chicago)
2602 North Clark Street
Lincoln Park
Chicago, IL 60614
773-883 -5101 docwinebar@aol.com
http://docwinebarchicago.com

Or
D.O.C Wine Bar (Lombard)
326 Yorktown Center
Lombard, IL
630-627-6666
www.docwinebarchicago.com/lombard

Designed with upscale cabin like affinities
with a handsome rustic exterior and a
swanky, classy interior, dressed in hardwood
floors, lofty ceilings and marble frills;
accented with passionate rosy lighting, cozy
couches and smooth tuneful music. This
place exudes romance in every aspect; add
in their extensive semi-global variety of
wines, delectable small plate appetizers and
burning fireplace and you've got one
enchanting and romantic evening.

 *Wine Bars*

WineStyles
1240 South Michigan Ave.
Chicago, IL 60605
312) 431-9999
www.winestyles.net/southloop

If you're a fan of imbibing the grape, you'll love this charming wine bar where you can bring your own food, listen to live music (Thursday & Fridays) and savor the multiple flavors of grapes from a variety of regions. Staged in old world wine cellar décor as hundreds of worldwide wine bottles protrude as props. They offer an extensive variety of wines categorized by flavor or taste rather than grape or region and are easily identifiable for any palate's desire.

Relax and mellow out in this composed vault of grapes. Winestyles wine bar is one of my favorite little escapes.

SEE COUPON SECTION FOR DISCOUNT

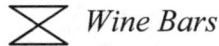 *Wine Bars*

Less Expensive Alternatives…..

Try an at home wine tasting where there is no corkage fee (a fee to drink wine in an establishment) or worry about driving afterwards.

Start by picking your wines narrow it down by reds, whites or both then decide the variety, choose by brand name, region, flavor (bold, sweet etc.) or grape (chardonnay, merlot, sauvignon blanc etc.) Choose five bottles to taste. You could also simply choose five different brand names and types of reds or whites or a combination of both to keep it simple.

Items needed:

❖ *4-5 bottles of chilled wine (45°F for whites and 55°F for red).*

❖ *4-6 wine glasses (you can choose to use two glasses if you are willing to continue rinsing between each tastings as oppose to every other).*

❖ *Ice water for rinsing the palates between tastings (bottled water will do but for a more romantic feel try a glass pitcher with separate water glasses).*

❖ *Additional palate cleansers: Cheese, crackers (unsalted), breads (no grain) nicely styled on a tray. Add Chocolates if desired.*

❖ *Small plates, napkins, 2 corkscrews (in case one breaks)*

❖ *Dumping bowl for unwanted wine*

❖ *Plastic waste cup for rinsing palate.*

❖ Table cloth (white is generally the better choice when dealing in reds to tell the color and intensity of the wine).

❖ Centerpiece: Pick up a glass bowl (specifically designed for a floating candle if possible). Insert some glass rocks red, clear or both to match the color of the wines of the evening. Add water and floating candles.

❖ Lighting: Dim lighting with a Pink or Red bulb with candles galore.

The Tasting

Describe your theme such as reds from France, the different brand names of merlot, sweet wines, bold wines or etc. Explain to your date what inspired you to select the wines of the evening.

Uncork and pour the wine into a glass at a 45° degree angle. Review the wine color depth.

Swirl the glass of wine to release the aromas. Then close your eyes and smell the glass of wine. What does is smell like (fruit, vegetables, etc)?

Swish a sip around in your mouth, what do you taste (berries, plum, etc).

Swallow slowly and think about the aftertaste.

Discussion: Like or dislikes, why or why not. (Feel free to use the wine grids on page 148-149).

Romantic Getaways

Chicago is home of an eclectic array of City Getaways, with comprehensive amenities for people with all desires.

Love is always bestowed as a gift -- freely, willingly, and without expectation.... We don't love to be loved; we love to love.
~ Leo Buscaglia

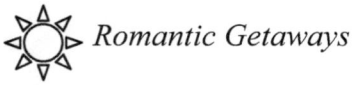 *Romantic Getaways*

Ambiance Suites

2955 Mannheim Road
Franklin Park, IL 60131
(847) 455-4070
www.ambiancesuites.com

Newest Location Opening Fall 2010
14400 S. Cicero Ave
Midlothian, IL

Embellished in high-end décor with luxury amenities, its name speaks for itself. Ambiance Suites offers an array of cutting-edge suites to choose from, equipped with steam & spa showers, incandescent fireplaces, oversized tubs and much more to take you and your date on a romantic, stimulating retreat you'll always remember.

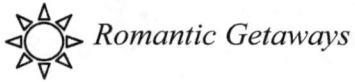

The Champagne Lodge
16 W62 S. Frontage Road
Willowbrook, IL 60527
(630) 455-0555
www.champagnelodge.com

Nicely styled in current design; you're sure
to find a hidden treasure in this gold mine.
Relax in the marbled steam room or the ultra
whirlpool tub; either tool will stimulate
renewal. Set in a sophisticated environment
with amenities galore that are sure to have
you and your date coming back for more.

Inquire about their additional packages and
products to amplify your stay.

The sprinkles Package: A satisfying
indulgence with an assortment of favors to
suit all. A gift basket containing a bottle of
champagne, two signature champagne flutes,
assorted scented candles, candies, cookies,
gourmet cupcakes and chocolate covered
strawberries.

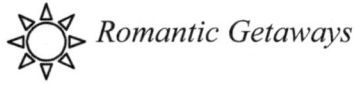

Sybaris

There are four locations throughout the Chicago land area to choose from.

Please visit the website for hours, locations and contact information nearest you.

630-960-4000
Downers Grove, IL
www.sybaris.com

You're sure to feel like a pearl when you escape into the pleasures of this exquisite, rare clam. The Sybaris houses swimming pool and whirlpool suites, satisfying to all your senses. With beautiful enhancements and handsome décor, you're sure to have a sultry, sexy night to be remembered. Take a vapor bath in the hot and heavy steam room; immerse your bodies in the swirling waters of a whirlpool tub or slide down the board of ecstasy into the swimming pool of paradise and then retire to your resting place with soft night light under glows atop pillows and linens as soft as marshmallows.

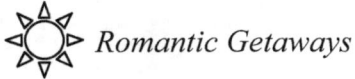

China Doll Guest House
738 West Schubert Avenue
Chicago, IL 60614
773-525-4967 or 866-361-1819
www.chinadollguesthouse.com

There are three locations to choose from around the Chicago land area. Visit their website or call for additional information.

Enjoy a home away from home feel with upgraded amenities this place really seals the deal. Accessorized with a steam room, fireplace, Jacuzzi and so forth, the extra buck or two this place is really worth. Feel at ease on the outside deck or take a view of the private garden, release your body of stress and give your mind a needed pardon. The outside is landscaped softly to calm, you'll never want to leave your home away from home.

Prepare your own breakfast in your private gourmet kitchen. The fridge is pre-stocked with all your needed fixings.

SEE COUPON SECTION FOR DISCOUNT

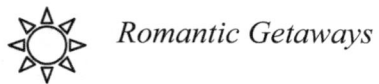

Sofitel Chicago Water Tower Luxury Hotel

20 East Chestnut Street (downtown)
Chicago, IL 60611
312-324-4000
www.sofitel.com

Visit one of Chicago's many attractions including Museums, Lake Michigan and Navy Pier, all within close proximity of this sleek, modernistic, upscale hotel. Sofitel Chicago has great accommodations as well as a luxurious design with a warm yet elegant feel and contemporary plush furnishings with bold colorful intentions. They offer an ultra modern dining experience and bar. The views from the rooms are breathtaking and overlook a radiantly ablaze Chicago at night.

Upgrade your room for one with a Jacuzzi tub; a more intimate way to show your love.

Enjoy an evening amongst the city aglow, walking hand and hand with your beau, giving romance a chance to bestow.

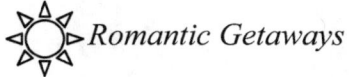 *Romantic Getaways*

Less Expensive Alternative……..

    *Some things are worth the extra buck or two; I recommend **No** skimping when it comes to getting away for some healing and fulfilling. Not only will you connect or reconnect with your special someone, it also proposes rejuvenation, stimulation, and exhilaration. My suggestions is to save $48.00 a month which breaks down to $12.00 a week for twelve months (if you have a cooperating partner, go half and have a retreat jar that you both contribute $6.00 a week). That should give you at least a two nights stay once or twice a year. So brown bag it once or twice a week for a revitalizing, invigorating, galvanizing retreat.*

Scenic Drives

Explore the wonders of man and nature throughout Chicagoland.

*The courses of true love never
did run smooth.
~ by William Shakespeare*

Lakeshore Drive
U.S. ROUTE 41
Starting from Ardmore to 71st Street
Chicago IL

Take an 18-mile drive along Chicago's stunning, pictorial lake front, where you'll encounter curvy roads, green parks, sand filled beaches, museums, skyscrapers, and Lake Michigan to name a few. There are adventures around every bend, use caution as you attend.

May I have this ride?
Take me by the hand and lead me on an excursion of ecstasy through Chicagoland. Hold on tight as you move about; the curves on her body will start to fill out. As you look around, the waves rippling from the sea of love are abound; Move about slowly so not to miss a beat as I gaze into your eyes, I feel the warmth of the sun's heat. I love your shape and your warm embrace but mostly how you make my heart race and the smile appear on my face.

~ Adrienne Hatton Mack~

 *Scenic Drives*

Chicago Neighborhood Tours
Chicago, IL
312-742-7530
info@chicagoofficeoftourism.org
www.chicagoneighborhoodtours.com

Origination Point:
Chicago Cultural Center
(Randolph Street Entrance)
77 East Randolph Street
Chicago, IL 60620

Take a guided journey by motor coach and foot into some of Chicago's momentous neighborhoods. Travel back in time, learning the ethnic, cultural, and educational factual heritage of several Chicago neighborhoods. Showcasing the vitality and exuberance of the communities from beautiful Beverly, know for historic homes, beautiful parks and churches, to Historical Bronzeville where you will learn about the African American cultural background.

The Magnificent Mile
Starting Point:
 300 North Michigan Ave
Chicago, IL 60611
312-642-3570
www.themagnificentmile.com

Embark upon eight blocks of VA-VA-VA-VOOM!!! Enjoy exquisite hotels, fine dining restaurants, charming boutiques, outstanding architecture and other peerless amenities of Chicago's Magnificent mile.

Rent a luxury car to enhance your experience...

Chicago Exotic Car Rentals
29 S. La Salle St. Suite 600
Chicago, IL 60603
 866.661.1054
www.chicagoexoticrentals.com

Renting luxury cars, sport cars, SUV's and exotic cars from Rolls Royce (with a driver), Aston Martin, Lamborghini, Bentley, Porsche, BMW, Mercedes, Escalade, Range Rover and Corvettes. Upgrade any of your scenic drives for the ride of a lifetime.

Less Expensive Alternative.....

*Prepare for an excursion in the comforts
of your own home. Buy a fascinating,
eventful DVD of Chicago that captivates
the city's history, architectural wonders,
luxurious landscapes, rivers and other
heavenly treasures.*

Purchase Location:

*The Chicago Museum of History
1601 N. Clark St.
Chicago, IL 60611
312.799.2262
www.chicagomuseumstore.org*

Sweets for my Sweets

Put the icing on the cake…Try some of
Chicago's melt in your mouth, decadent to
die for, intimate dessert spots.

The most eloquent silence; that of two
mouths meeting in a sweet kiss.
~ by Unknown

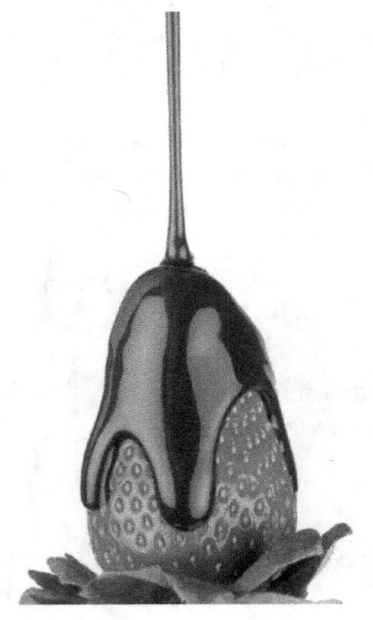

Eli's Cheesecake World & Cafe
6701 W Forest Preserve Ave
Chicago, IL 60634
(773) 205-3800 or 800-354-2253
www.elicheesecake.com

This place puts the oomph in Cheesecakes,
offering a variety from key lime breeze and
chocolate chip to mud pie. These delectable
delicacies you really must try.

Decorated with baked goods as fixtures and
celebrity wall murals as art, the desserts are
to die for, sure to steal your heart.

Take the tour and have some fun; from crust
to décor you'll see how it's done.

Get better acquainted over dessert, feed her
cheesecake as a way to flirt.

Sweets for my Sweets

Hershey's Chicago
822 North Michigan Avenue
Chicago, IL 60611-2166
(312) 337-7711
www.hersheys.com/discover/chicago

Craving for chocolate? Look no further; full
of wall to wall cocoa bursting out the door.
Be amused while you wait for personalized
chocolate for your date. Compose a
message to be attached to a giant 7oz.
Hershey's kiss, guaranteed to skyrocket any
mood from sorrow to bliss. Try
personalizing a giant chocolate bar
To say how you feel ensuring ones wounded
heart properly heals. Whatever the occasion
include chocolate in the equation.

Chocolates are like fine art; a master piece
created from the heart. A token of affection,
a symbol of love; a euphoric feeling sent
down from the heavens above.

Hot Chocolate Dessert Bar

1747 North Damen Avenue
Chicago, IL 60647
(773) 489-1747
www.hotchocolatechicago.com

Chocoholics rejoice..... Ravished in chocolate hues and sophisticated chocolaty appeal as perfumes of chocolate breeze the air in this sensual, toasty haven.

Their hot cocoa is a succulent delight, served with hot fudge, hot chocolate and home-made marshmallows, giving off immediate intoxicating aromas.

Delectable desserts encompass the menu starting with chocolate. Warm chocolate soufflé tart, salted caramel ice cream and home-made pretzels; Warm Brioche Doughnuts- served with hot fudge.
Ice Cream and Sorbet Flight- a tasting of freshly made ice creams and sorbets. Choose up to eight a great dessert to share with your date.

The Plush Horse
12301 S 86th Ave
Palos Park, IL 60464
(708) 761-6979
www.theplushhorse.com

Like your dessert cold and frozen? For all
ice cream fanatics or people who just can't
resist good ole fashion ice cream, The Plush
Horse is the place to visit. Designed in
reminiscent of an old ice cream parlor with
strawberry colored walls, tin ceilings and
counter tops, hardwood floors and charm in
abundance; bringing back pleasant
memories of yester years. Serving vast
arrays of homemade ice cream to choose
from, beginning with chocolate cherry kiss,
apple pie, black cherry, Hawaiian delight,
pumpkin pie, watermelon, pistachio and
peppermint to start. The inside seating is
nice; however I prefer the outside courtyard.

Jimmy Jamm Sweet Potato Pie
1844 W. 95th Street
Chicago, IL 60643
773-779-9105

YUM, YUM, YUM or should I say YAM, YAM, YAM.....this place is a sweet potato paradise. Serving sweet potato scones, sweet potato cupcakes, sweet potato pies, sweet potato cakes, sweet potato muffins, sweet potato cookies, sweet potato turn over's, sweet potato ice cream and more, this place has gone sweet potato galore.

Abstract art adorns the walls conjoined with Painted hues of orange, peach and gold; however it's a quiet effect by no means is it bold.

Immerse yourself in the fascination of the pastry chef preparing dessert, or repose at an intimate table with plush seating designed for comfort.

In a pleasant, friendly atmosphere where the staff is nice and endear; assure to bring a date, and take home a souvenir.

SEE COUPON SECTION FOR DISCOUNT

Less Expensive Alternative....

Add a zing to any night...Make her a sweet treat.
If your date is a chocoholic try making her some Milk Chocolate Popcorn
Ingredients:
6 cups of popped popcorn
1 ¼ cups of salted peanuts
½ package of milk chocolate morsels
½ cup of light corn syrup
2 Tablespoons of butter or margarine

Directions:
Preheat oven to 300 degrees F
Grease a roasting pan

Combine popcorn and nuts in roasting pan. Combine morsels, corn syrup & butter in a heavy duty saucepan, cook over medium heat stirring constantly, until mixture boils. Pour over popcorn and toss well to coat all kernels. Bake for 30-40 minutes stirring frequently. Let cool before serving.

25 Questions to ask on a date

New love or old, communication brings about memories to unfold.

Look into her eyes as you listen to her soul; unlock the inner most thoughts and desires to be told.

The more you talk the more you know; watering the seed for the relationship to grow.

Although a key component, conversation may not always be the easiest task but the benefits reaped your sure to bask. Here is a list of questions to ask……

Adrienne Hatton-Mack

25 Questions to ask on a date

1. *If you could pick one, what was the best day you ever had? Why?*

2. *When you were a child what did you want to be when you grew up?*

3. *What is your biggest weakness?*

4. *Who is or was your inspiration and why?*

5. *What is currently your biggest fear?*

6. *What's your favorite animal? What's so intriguing about it?*

7. *Do you give to a charity? Which one? If not, what charity would you want to donate to?*

8. *What countries have you visited? Or which country would you like to visit?*

9. *What's your favorite past time?*

10. *What's most important to you right now?*

11. *Do you have any aspirations? If so what are they?*

12. *What is your fondest childhood memory?*

13. *What is the most pain you've ever experienced? Physical or emotional?*

14. *What qualities do you most treasure in your best friend?*

15. *What's the best decision you've ever made?*

16. *If you could change anything about your up-bringing, what would it be?*

17. *If you could have any job in the world, what would it be?*

18. *What places (cities) would you like to visit? What would you do there?*

19. *What is the most adventurous thing you've done?*

20. *What are you most passionate about?*

21. *What is important in a relationship to you?*

22. *If you could change something about yourself, what would it be and why?*

23. *On a scale of 1-10 how important is love to you?*

24. *What achievements are you most proud of?*

25. *If you had one day in your life that you could live over, which day would it be and why?*

Quality Time Together

*Quality time is a token well treasured;
yet for some reason the jewel remains
buried. An essential for romance and
love altogether, time taken may be the
element for the tether.*

Adrienne Hatton-Mack

See a Play Together
Broadway in Chicago

Cadillac Palace Theatre
151 W. Randolph Street
Chicago, IL 60602
312-384-1502 Theatre direct
800-775-2000 Ticket master
www.broadwayinchicago.com

Stop by the box office to purchase tickets or call ticket master.

Visit their website for performances, show times, additional theatres and general information.

Get fancied up or go casual to see romance enacted on stage....steal slight glances to watch her reactions as she stays eagerly engaged.

Take a wine making class together

Bevart Brewer & Winemaking
10033 South Western Avenue
Chicago, IL 60643
(773) 233-7579
www.bev-art.com

Let the juices of romance start to flow as the seeds of love begin to grow. Learn to make your own wine; the drink preferred by the Gods above; the renowned worldwide drink of Love.

Take a Couple's Cooking Class

Parties That Cook
1000 W. Washington Blvd.
Chicago, IL
888-907-COOK (2665)
www.partiesthatcook.com

Have a fascinating, educational evening learning to cook. You will interactively work on a recipe of an array of preselected menu items, and then retire to sit down and dine...for an added bonus, bring a bottle of wine.

Time for Pickings...Go fruit picking

Garden Patch Farms & Orchard
14154 W. 159th Street
Homer Glen, IL 60491
708-301-7720
www.gardenpatchfarms.com

Open June-October for Picking

Bake him a pie after apple picking.
Attach a note saying:

Thank you for a wonderful day of apple picking...now treat yourself to some finger licking (pie of course).

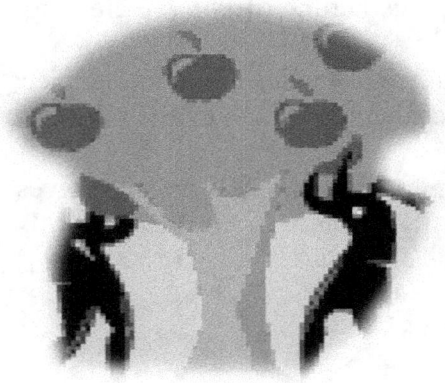

Go Ice Skating Together

McCormick Tribune Ice Skating Rink
55 North Michigan Ave.
Chicago, IL 60602
312-742-5222
www.millenniumpark.org
Open: November-March

Visit their website or call for season and
time of operation is subject to change
without notice.

Amongst beautiful downtown Chicago is
where you'll be ice skating… a romantic
moment together the two of you creating.

Hold her hand as you glide across the ice;
stop to steal a kiss or two to add more spice.

Help her up when she falls down; it gives
her security in knowing you're around.

Take a Couple's Massage Class

Graceland Western Massage
Chicago, IL
773-386-0547
www.gracelandwestmassage.com
Origination Point:
1599 Maple Ave
Evanston, IL 60201

Learn how to caress each other from head to toe. This 90 minute class teaches you what you need to know. It will also help with my section on massage!

SEE COUPON SECTION FOR DISCOUNT

Blues, Blues, and More Blues

Kingston Mines Blues Club
2548 North Halsted Street
Chicago, IL 60614
773-477-4646
http://www.kingstonmines.com

Hear the sounds of heart pounding, hand
clapping, feet stomping live rhythm and
blues musicians seven nights a week in this
cozy and chummy spot. Revel in the
electrifying sounds and listen to the emotion
behind the song; listen for the endeavors for
which their hearts belong. Drink booze and
eat from a variety of southern food, at the
end of the night show your date affectionate
gratitude.

Take a couple's dance class together

May I Have This Dance
5246 North Elston 2nd Floor
Chicago, IL 60630
773-635-3000
www.mayihavethisdance.com

Absorb the knowledge and drink the energy
as you take a fascinating course in Dance
with lessons in Salsa, Latin, Swing, Hustle,
Ballroom, Steppin' and Hip Hop.

How About some Jazz!

Back Room Jazz Club
1007 N Rush Street
Chicago, IL
312-751-2433/2434
www.backroomchicago.com

Prepare to indulge in a wonderful night of
Jazz together. Murals of musicians liven up
the walls as candles lighten up the small
intimate tables and bar in a mellow, swank
atmosphere.

Listen while the live musicians express
themselves through song; if you know the
tune, silently hum along.

 I highly recommend securing reservations
to ensure you're able to get a nice table.

Visit The Aquarium

The Shedd Aquarium
1200 South Lake Shore Drive
Chicago, IL 60605
(312)939-2438

Watch the courting and playing of the
underworld. Watch as they swirl, whirl, curl
and twirl.

Go Horseback Riding Together

Forest View Farms
16717 S. Lockwood Ave.
Tinley Park, IL 60477
708-560-0306
www.fvfarms.com

Ride a horse around the trail; spontaneity
keeps love fresh from getting stale.

Enjoy nature while riding a horse… give
your date a wink and let romance take its
course.

Visit Willis Tower (aka Sears Tower)

The Skydeck
233 S. Wacker Drive suite 3530
Chicago, IL 60606
(Enter skydeck on Jackson blvd)
312-875-9696
www.the-skydeck.com

View Chicago like never before, from the
Willis Tower 103rd floor.

Take a Wine course together

Chicago Wine School
1942 South Halsted Street
Chicago, IL 60608
312-491-0284
www.wineschool.com

Chicago wine school will teach you how to get up close and personal with wine, how to educate your palate and what you need to know to be a good connoisseur of this love potion called wine.

Go to a bar…..Have a cocktail

The Violet Hour
1520 North Damen Avenue
Chicago, IL 60622
(773) 252-1500
www.thevioIethour.com

Talk the night away at this intimate, swanky cocktail lounge. Enclosed you'll find crystal chandeliers, cozy fireplace, and high backed leather chairs assembled around small white tables illuminated by candlelight.

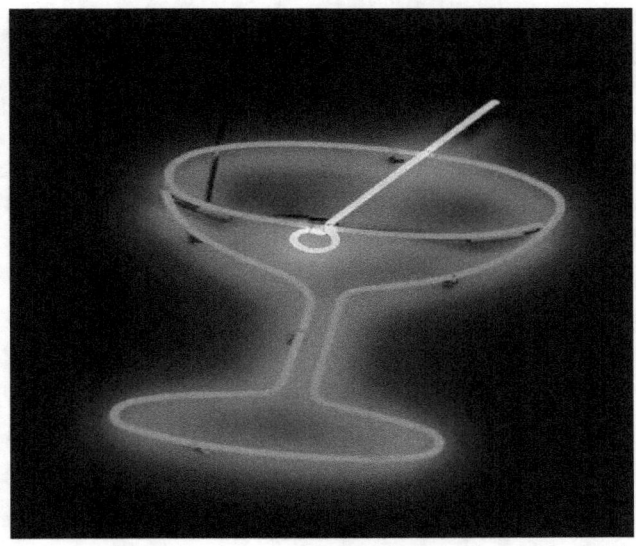

Go Bowling together

Don't stop now, keep the ball rolling...take it to the lanes, let's go bowling.

Lucky Strikes Lanes & Lounge
322 E. Illinois Street
Chicago, IL 60611
312.245.8331
www.bowlluckystrike.com

Ready, set, let the games begin....
Lucky Strikes is an up-scale bowling alley with a classy feel, serving adults 21 and older drinks at the bar and a good meal. Let loose and go bowling, have a meal, shoot pool, or watch TV on the big screens. Whatever your pleasure your experience will be keen.

Go to a Museum together...

Chicago is home to a great selection of distinctive museums. Enter some of the most profoundly moving depositories of history and art Chicago has to offer. Take a leisurely stroll while educating your mind and nourish your soul.

Museum Of Science and Industry
57th & Lake Shore Drive
Chicago, IL 60637
(773) 684-1414
www.msichicago.org

Admire the Collection of brilliant modules and enjoy the creative hands on exhibits detailing science and Technology.

Quality Time Together

The Art Institute of Chicago Museum
111 South Michigan Avenue
Chicago, IL 60603
(312)443-3600
www.artic.edu

See love portrayed on sculptures and canvas
depicting the affections of artists and
civilizations around the world.

The Chicago History Museum
1601 N. Clark Street
Chicago, IL 60614
(312)642-4600
www.chicagohs.org

See the intimate details on Chicago's
historical past events, present success
and future endeavors.

Dusable Museum
740 East 56th Street
Chicago, IL 60637
(773)947-0600
www.dusablemuseum.org

See African American cultural exhibits of
love, struggles and accomplishments.

The Adler Planetarium
1300 S. Lake Shore Drive
Chicago, IL 60605
312-922-STAR (7827)

Watch the stars and the worlds above; enjoy
the experience with your beloved.

Show them that you care

Throughout all life's struggles and strife's, don't forget to STOP for LOVE....In its highest regard the component that makes life worth it.

Adrienne Hatton-Mack

Show them that you care

Photo Blanket

Custom Creations Unlimited, Inc.
20 Danada Square West, #181
Wheaton, Illinois 60189
630-665-1969
www.original-photo-blankets.com

Create a blanket with a photo of you...
attach a note saying:

***Whenever you're cold; I'll be here to keep
you warm.***

SEE COUPON SECTION FOR DISCOUNT

Send a singing telegram

Fantastic Fantasies
Chicago, IL
800-762-8863
http://www.balloonogram.com

Send her a song symbolic of your relationship. You can never go wrong sending a love song.

SEE COUPON SECTION FOR DISCOUNT

Message In A Bottle

The Kemper Lake Group
815-609-9550
800-747-8304
www.onepassionplace.com

Send your relationship into full throttle by sending them a message in a bottle.

Show them that you care

Give him/her a Phuzzle (Photo Puzzle) of the two of you

PersonalizationMall.com
51 Shore Drive
Burr Ridge, IL 60527
630-910-6000
www.personalizationmall.com/

Attach a note saying:

No matter how broken the pieces...we always manage to put ourselves back together again.

Decorate his/her yard for any occasion

Flamingo Surprise
250 James Street
Bensenville, IL 60106
630-350-1280
http://www.flamingosurprise.com

Decorate his yard; it's a twist to giving him a card….say how you feel in a big way to celebrate your special man all day.

SEE COUPON SECTION FOR DISCOUNT

Show them that you care

Get a personalized T-shirt made for him/her

T-Shirt Deli
1739 North Damen Avenue
Chicago, IL 60647
(773) 276-6266
www.tshirtdeli.com

Say what you mean on a T-shirt…an expressive way to keep your feelings close to their heart.

Custom music keepsake box

Things Remembered
210 Chicago Ridge Mall
Chicago Ridge, IL 60415
(708) 499-1010
www.thingsremembered.com
Visit their website for additional locations

Create a music box with your song and thoughts of her....showing her how you feel makes her feel secure.

Customize Fortune Cookies

Awesome Creations Incorporated
150 S. Washington Street – Suite E
Carpentersville, IL 60110
847-428-8828 or 877-729-3766
www.awesomecreations.com

Dipped in chocolate and covered in
sprinkles, a surprise gift to make their eyes
twinkle. Personalize the message inside;
have them shipped to where she resides.

Show them that you care

Customize a Fragrance

Aroma Workshop
2050 N Halsted Street
Chicago, IL 60614
(773) 871-1985
www.aromaworkshop.com

Create a perfume with scents from the heart; customize your creation like a work of art.

Bake cookies

Write a reason you like/love him/her on each cookie……attach a note saying the reasons you like/love them.

Show them that you care

Personalized Trophies

Awards International/Chicago Trophy Co
6333 West Howard Street
Niles, Illinois 60714
800-621-8826
773-685-8200
www.awardsco.com

Give them an achievement award statue with
a # one rate, in recognition of being and
outstanding mate.   You can personally
engrave; I'd bet by far the best gift you ever
gave.

Show Them you Care by building them a bear!!!

Build –A- Bear Workshop
700 E Grand Avenue
Chicago, IL 60611
312-832-0114
www.***buildabear***.com

Build her a bear with resemblances to you…

Attach a note saying***:*** ***Hold me close, Hold me tight; hold me for comfort all through the night.***

Put on a Lingerie Fashion Show

Victoria Secrets
332 Orland Square Dr
Orland Park, IL 60462
708-403-2911
www.victoriassecret.com
Visit their website for locations
nearest you.

Strut your stuff as he watches in glee; use
different props to act a little flirty (or dirty).

*Love sometimes causes pain, but
Sunshine comes after the stormy rain;
drizzle down some romance and love
will shine through.*

Adrienne Hatton-Mack

*Give Love Coupons good for
recreating a memorable experience
you had from this book.*

THIS COUPON ENTITLES YOU TO A

ROMANTIC DINNER

OFFER GOOD FOR ETERNITY

THIS COUPON ENTITLES YOU TO A

BED & BREAKFAST GETAWAY

OFFER GOOD FOR ETERNITY

THIS COUPON ENTITLES YOU TO A

DINNER & MOVIE THEATRE

OFFER GOOD FOR ETERNITY

THIS COUPON ENTITLES YOU TO A

ROMANTIC CHICAGO TOUR

OFFER GOOD FOR ETERNITY

THIS COUPON ENTITLES YOU TO A

SPA TREATMENT

OFFER GOOD FOR ETERNITY

THIS COUPON ENTITLES YOU TO A

ROMANTIC GETAWAY

OFFER GOOD FOR ETERNITY

THIS COUPON ENTITLES YOU TO A

ROMANTIC 1 HOUR MASSAGE

OFFER GOOD FOR ETERNITY

THIS COUPON ENTITLES YOU TO A

ROMANTIC DESSERT OUTING

OFFER GOOD FOR ETERNITY

THIS COUPON ENTITLES YOU TO A

ROMANTIC AIR ADVENTURE

OFFER GOOD FOR ETERNITY

THIS COUPON ENTITLES YOU TO A

ROMANTIC DAY OF PAMPERING

OFFER GOOD FOR ETERNITY

THIS COUPON ENTITLES YOU TO A

ROMANTIC WINE BAR OUTING

OFFER GOOD FOR ETERNITY

THIS COUPON ENTITLES YOU TO A

ROMANTIC OUTING OF CHOICE

OFFER GOOD FOR ETERNITY

THIS COUPON ENTITLES YOU TO A

ROMANTIC @ HOME SPA

OFFER GOOD FOR ETERNITY

THIS COUPON ENTITLES YOU TO A

ROMANTIC SCENIC DRIVE

OFFER GOOD FOR ETERNITY

THIS COUPON ENTITLES YOU TO A

ROMANTIC GIFT

OFFER GOOD FOR ETERNITY

THIS COUPON ENTITLES YOU TO A

ROMANTIC PICINIC OUTING

OFFER GOOD FOR ETERNITY

JIMMY JAMM SWEET POTATO CAFE

THIS COUPON ENTITLES YOU TO

$2.00 OFF A SWEET POTATOE PIE

OFFER EXPIRES 12/30/2011

Not Valid with Any Other Coupons/promotions

LYNFRED WINERY

THIS COUPON ENTITLES YOU TO A

FREE WINE TASTING FOR 2

OFFER EXPIRES 12/30/2011

Not Valid with Any Other
Coupons/promotions

HARVEY HOUSE BED & BREAKFAST

THIS COUPON ENTITLES YOU TO A

BOTTLE OF WINE & CHOCOLATE COVERED
STRAWBERRIES WITH A Stay

OFFER EXPIRES 12/30/2011

Not Valid with Any other Coupons/promotions

TOMMY GUN'S GARAGE

THIS COUPON ENTITLES YOU TO A

$5.00 OFF DISCOUNT

OFFER EXPIRES 12/30/2011

Not Valid with Any other coupons/promotions

COOPERS HAWK WINERY
& RESTAURANT

THIS COUPON ENTITLES YOU TO A
FREE WINE TASTING FOR 2
Tasting Room Only

OFFER EXPIRES 12/30/2011

Not Valid with any other coupons/promotions

POPS FOR CHAMPAGNE

THIS COUPON ENTITLES YOU TO A

2 FOR 1 GLASS OF SPARKLING WINE

OFFER EXPIRES 12/30/2011

Not Valid with any other coupons/promotions

VEOLA´S DAY SPA

THIS COUPON ENTITLES YOU TO A

20% DISCOUNT OFF COUPLE'S
LOVE & HAPPINESS PACKAGE

OFFER EXPIRES 12/30/2011

Not Valid with any other coupons/promotions

WINESTYLES SOUTH LOOP

THIS COUPON ENTITLES YOU TO A

10% OFF PURCHASE
@WINESTYLE SOUTH LOOP LOCATION
ONLY

OFFER EXPIRES 12/30/2011

Not Valid with any other coupons/promotions

CHINA DOLL GUEST HOUSE

THIS COUPON ENTITLES YOU TO A

$100.00 DISCOUNT OFF 3 NIGHTS
STAY

OFFER EXPIRES 12/30/2011

Not Valid with any other coupons/promotions

GRACELAND WESTERN MASSAGE

THIS COUPON ENTITLES YOU TO A

10% DISCOUNT OFF COUPLES
LESSON

OFFER EXPIRES 12/30/2011

Not Valid with any other coupons/promotions

GEJA´S CAFE

THIS COUPON ENTITLES YOU TO A

$25.00 OFF PURCHASE OF 2
PREMIER DINNERS

OFFER EXPIRES 12/30/2011

Not Valid with any other coupons/promotions

Palwaukee Flyers/Chicago
Executive Flight School

THIS COUPON ENTITLES YOU TO A

10% DISCOUNT OFF THE LAKE
GENEVA GETAWAY FLIGHT

OFFER EXPIRES 12/30/2011

Not Valid with any other coupons/promotions

WINDY CITY MASSAGE

THIS COUPON ENTITLES YOU TO A

$40.00 DISCOUNT OFF COUPLES
MASSAGE

OFFER EXPIRES 12/30/2011

Not Valid with any other coupons/promotions

FLAMINGO SURPRISE

THIS COUPON ENTITLES YOU TO

$20.00 OFF ANY DISPLAY

OFFER EXPIRES 12/30/2011

Not Valid with any other coupons/promotions

FANTASTIC FANTASIES

THIS COUPON ENTITLES YOU TO A

$5.00 OFF SINGING TELEGRAM OR
BALLOONS BOUQUET ORDER

OFFER EXPIRES 12/30/2011

Not Valid with any other coupons/promotions

CUSTOM CREATIONS UNLIMITED

THIS COUPON ENTITLES YOU TO

$5.00 OFF A CUSTOMIZED BLANKET

OFFER EXPIRES 12/30/2011

MENTION CODE AMB210
Not Valid with any other coupons/promotions

Wine Tasting Grid

	1	2	3	4	5
Wine Name					
Color & intensity					
Aroma					
Flavor, Acidity, sweetness					
Tannins, Body, Alcohol					
Finish & Complexity					
Do You like It?					

Wine Tasting Grid

	1	2	3	4	5
Wine Name					
Color & intensity					
Aroma					
Flavor, Acidity, sweetness					
Tannins, Body, Alcohol					
Finish & Complexity					
Do You like It?					

For ordering information,
please email your requests to
romancearoundchicagoland@hotmail.com

www.ingramcontent.com/pod-product-compliance
Lightning Source LLC
Chambersburg PA
CBHW060112260626
47160CB00005B/1872